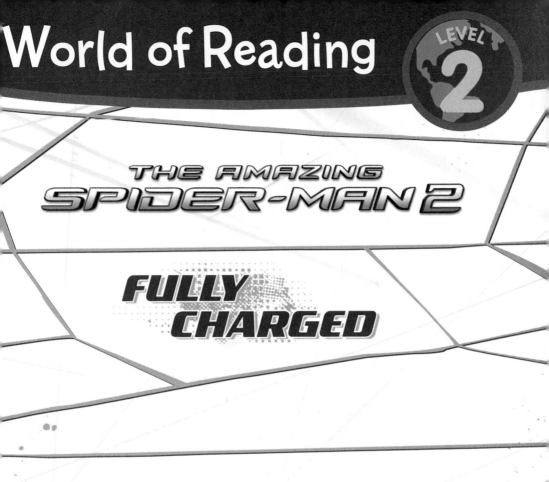

THE AMAZING SPIDER-MAN 2

FULLY CHARGED

WRITTEN BY BRITTANY CANDAU

BASED ON THE SCREENPLAY BY ALEX KURTZMAN & ROBERTO ORCI & JEFF PINKNER

PRODUCED BY AVI ARAD AND MATT TOLMACH

DIRECTED BY MARC WEBB

ILLUSTRATED BY ANDY SMITH, DREW GERACI, AND PETE PANTAZIS

MARVEL

New York • Los Angeles

 © MARVEL marvelkids.com © 2014 CPII

Printed in the United States of America

First Edition

1 3 5 7 9 10 8 6 4 2

Library of Congress Control Number: 2013955170

G658-7729-4-14046

ISBN 978-1-4231-9754-6

SUSTAINABLE FORESTRY INITIATIVE

Certified Chain of Custody
Promoting Sustainable Forestry

www.sfiprogram.org
SFI-01415

The SFI label applies to the text stock

Spider-Man is a Super Hero.

He crawls on walls.

He also swings from webs.

Spider-Man chases bad guys.

It is a tough job.

Spidey's real name is Peter Parker.

Peter lives with Aunt May.

He has to keep his Super Hero

identity a secret!

But that is not easy.

Aunt May doesn't always knock.

Our hero keeps an eye on the city.

He sees his friend down below.

Her name is Gwen Stacy.

Gwen is really smart.

She works at Oscorp.

Max Dillon also worked at Oscorp.

But he had an accident.

Now he wants to hurt people.

So he became a villain.

He calls himself Electro!

Electro has a lot of power.

He uses electricity.

He can shoot bolts from his hands.

He can even float in the air!

He uses his powers for evil.

Spidey once tried to help Electro.

He told him he could be a good guy.

Electro had the choice to use his

powers for good.

Electro thought about what Spidey

said.

Electro still wanted to be a bad guy.

Electro blasted Spidey

into a car!

This made Spider-Man mad.

The battle was on!

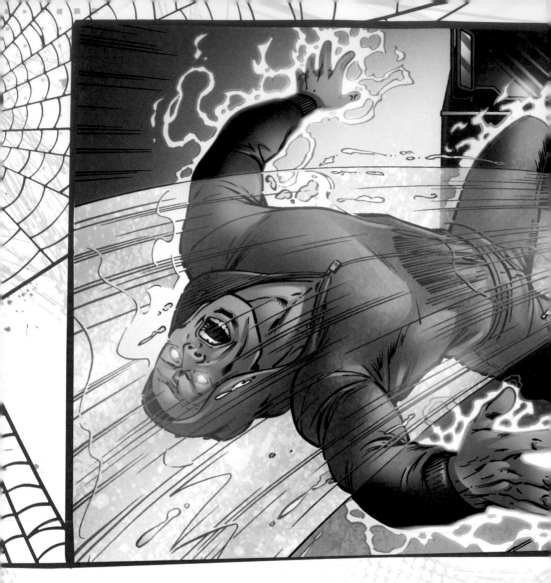

Spider-Man finds
Electro's weakness.
Spider-Man looks at the
fire hose.

What doesn't mix well

with electricity?

Water!

Electro is defeated . . . for now.

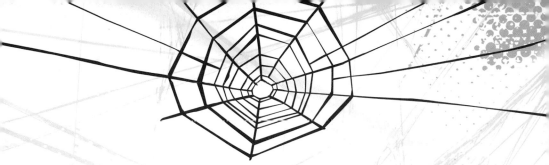

Uh-oh!

Electro has recharged.

And he plans to make trouble again!

"I'll take away all the power

in the city!" he says.

All the lights turn off.

All the TVs turn off.

All the radios

and all the computers turn off, too.

The city goes very dark.

Only one person can save the day.

His name is Spider-Man!

Gwen gives the hero a great idea.

Electro can't handle too much power.

Spidey charges his web-shooters.

He goes to find the Super Villain.

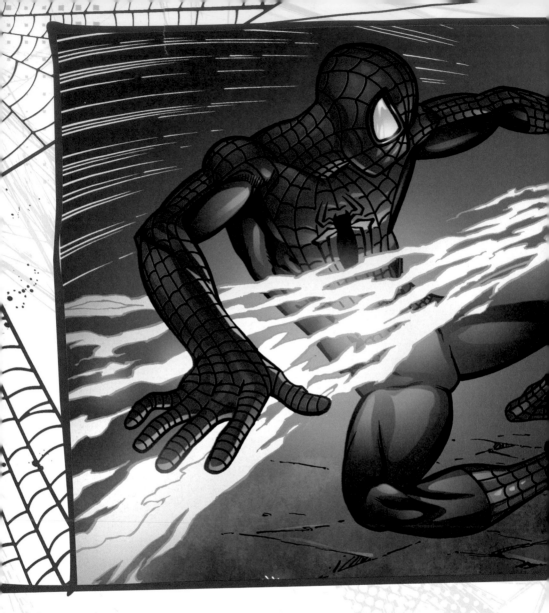

Electro is not happy.

Spidey is interrupting his plans!

He fires electricity at Spider-Man.

Spider-Man dodges Electro's blasts.

He shoots a web at the Super Villain.

Electro lunges at Spider-Man,
and Spidey ducks out of the way.
It is time to put Electro
on full blast!

It works! Electro surges

with too much electricity.

He shakes and shorts out.

It is bye-bye, Electro!

Spider-Man looks out

at the bright city beneath him.

He brought power

back to the people.

And saved the day again.

Being Spider-Man is not easy.
But he likes helping people
and defeating the bad guys.
And Spidey would not have it
any other way!